Toad and Bug came
up the road.
"I see a fine coat,"
said Toad.

The coat was on the
line.
"I like this coat,"
said Toad.

Toad got the coat.
The coat fit him.

"It is not nice to take the coat," said Bug. "It is mine," said Toad.

"It is not," said Bug.
"It is no joke to
take a coat."

Toad gave Bug a poke.
"I am a fine toad in
a fine coat," said
Toad.

Toad and Bug came to
a lake.
Toad got up on the
oak log.

"I am a fine toad in a
fine coat," said Toad.
"I do not see a fine
toad," said Bug.

"I can hop, hop, hop,"
said Toad.
"I am a fine toad in
a fine coat and I can
hop on a log."

But Toad fell off the
log into the mud.
He got mud on his
fine coat.

Toad got soap and a pail.
He got in the boat.
"The soap can get rid of
the mud on the coat,"
said Toad.

Toad had to dip the
coat in the pail.
The soap made a lot
of foam.
Toad had to rub and rub.

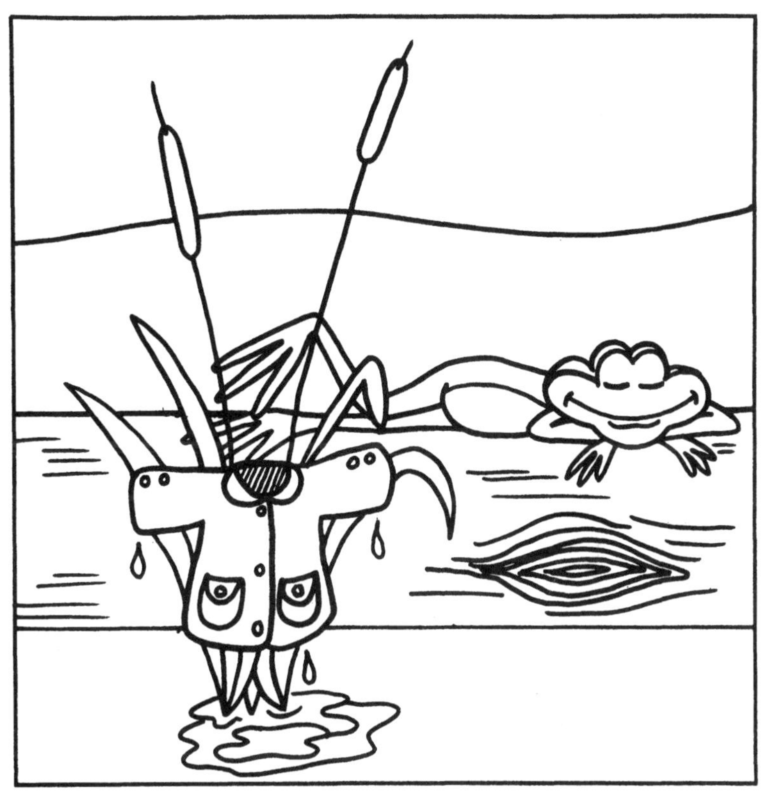

Toad set his wet coat
in the hot sun and got
up on the log to take
a nap.

Toad woke up and ran
to get his coat.

The coat was not wet,
but it did not fit him.
The sad toad gave a
big moan.

"I see a big, sad toad
in a coat made to fit
a bug," said Bug.